FARMER PALMER'S WAGON RIDE

Story and Pictures by William Steig

A Sunburst Book

Farrar, Straus and Giroux

TO MAGGIE, MELINDA, FRANCESCA, HAL, AND BUTCH

An hour before sunrise, Farmer Palmer tip-hoofed out of the house and went to the barn to wake up his hired hand, Ebenezer.

He lighted a lantern and hooked it to a post on his loaded wagon
while Ebenezer, mumbling as he often did, got into harness, buckling
most of the straps himself. Then Farmer Palmer leaped up on the seat
and set out for the market to sell his leeks, turnips, and lettuce.

About eight o'clock they rolled into town, Ebenezer plodding, nodding, and staring at the ground through his thick glasses. By ten, all the vegetables had been sold. Farmer Palmer's pockets bulged with money and he spent some of it on presents for his family. For his fine, fat wife he bought a camera. For his fat son Mack, who liked to build things, he bought a tool chest; for his fat daughter Maria, a bicycle, because she'd been wanting one; and for his fat son Zeke, who was musical, a harmonica. For his fat self he got a silver watch, and for old Ebenezer, who was subject to sunstroke, a straw hat to keep the sun from toasting his noggin.

Ebenezer hadn't expected a present. "Swish my tail!" he murmured bashfully as he hugged Farmer Palmer to his furry chest.

They started homeward at noon, having drunk quarts of sarsaparilla to quench their thirst. If all went well—and why shouldn't it?—they'd be back at the farm by three o'clock, as Farmer Palmer had promised.

It was August and the hot sun glittered through a haze. They chatted as they moved along. Ebenezer opined that rain would have a cooling effect, and Farmer Palmer was of the same opinion.

Then they were both silent and listened to the zizzing-zazzing, chirring-whirring of the heat-charged insects. Farmer Palmer mopped his hot head with a red rag and thought of home. He wanted to be back with his fine, fat family and watch their faces as they received their gifts.

In a while the road roughened and went through woods. As the wagon hobbled over the bumps, black clouds assembled and cast the earth in shadow. Harum-scarum gusts of wind turned the leaves this way and that. Then the rain they had hoped for came, with scattered drops as big as acorns slapping down, followed by a drubbing deluge.

The road's dust disappeared and the world swam in water. Thunder rumbled, and rambled around in the distance. Then it came frightfully close. It dramberamberoomed. It bomBOMBED! A jagged knife of

lightning slashed through a tree. Ebenezer and the farmer, gawking up,
saw the tree descending on them and they were petrified with terror.
Both realized they would rather not die at that particular time.

The tree kept coming nevertheless and fell across the wagon, making it shudder, but miraculously neither the pig nor the ass was hurt. They were in a maze of branches and leaves and their wagon was clamped to the ground.

Farmer Palmer looked over at Ebenezer and up at the heavens and asked: "How am I ever going to get home to my loving wife and children?" Neither the ass nor the heavens answered. He disposed of his own question by reaching under some branches for his son Mack's tool chest and extracting a saw and ax.

"No one will ever believe this," said Ebenezer, undoing his traces. "Let's take a picture." He found Mrs. Palmer's camera, covered his head with the black cloth, and photographed the pig angrily chopping away. Then they both went to work hacking and sawing, with a thuck-thwuck and a whoosh-sheesh, whoosh-sheesh. In a couple of hours the tree was in pieces and the wagon was free. The rain had stopped and the sun shone. It was no cooler.

The tree had driven the wheels into mud and Ebenezer had to
stiffen his old legs and heave forward to get the wagon going again.
Farmer Palmer hoped there'd be no more delays. They were going to be
late as it was and he knew his family would be worrying.

They came to a steep grade that fell away for half a mile. Part way down, the wagon jolted and shook loose a nut that held one of the wheels to its axle. The wheel said goodbye to the wagon and raced down the hill, delighted to be on its own. Farmer Palmer jumped from his seat and went galloping after it.

"Please stop!" he yelled. "Please stop or I'll never ever get home. My wife and kids are waiting!" The wheel had no interest in Farmer Palmer's predicament. It leaped and jounced and tore along, and the exasperated pig could only tear after.

Farmer Palmer felt Zeke's harmonica bouncing about in his pocket. He yanked it out and, winded as he was from running, he managed to play a short tune, inbreathing some of the notes:

Rith-moo, zee-zoo,
Zee-zwee.
Zwaddle-braddle-doo.

The wheel stopped dead in its tracks to listen to these remarkable sounds. It quivered, ribbled and dibbled around, and lay down flat. Farmer Palmer seized it by the spokes, shook and scolded it, dragged it up the hill, and fastened it tight on its axle, while Ebenezer mumbled something about wheels with minds of their own. By now it was four o'clock.

"Do you think you could go any faster, Ebenezer?"

"I'm pretty tired."

"I know," said Farmer Palmer.

"Try hitting me a few flicks with the whip," Ebenezer suggested. "Not too gently, not too hard."

Farmer Palmer whomped the whip in the air, and snapped it lightly on the ass's rump. "Gee-up!" he whooped. Ebenezer broke into a trot, his hoofs clattering on the now dry road.

Farther along, Ebenezer's dim eyes spied a turtle. Swerving to avoid it, he caught his hoof in a hole, limped a few steps, then dropped on his haunches, braying with such pain that even the serene hills winced.

"What is it?" asked Farmer Palmer, hopping off the wagon.

"I believe I've sprained my hock," wailed Ebenezer. "Left hind leg." And he rebrayed his bray of pain.

"Does braying really help?" the pig asked impatiently. "Are you sure it's a sprain? Try standing up."

Ebenezer tried. "The pain won't let me."

He began to bray again but made it a grunt. "I don't know how you'll ever get home to your poor worried wife and children. Oh, I'm such an awkward ass! I'm ashamed of myself."

"Nonsense!" snapped Farmer Palmer. He somehow managed to get Ebenezer out of his harness and into the wagon.

The ass lay there staring as Farmer Palmer got between the shafts and fastened the harness on his own fat belly.

"Bats and barnacles!" Ebenezer exclaimed, taking a picture of the pig as beast of burden.

Farmer Palmer pulled and the wagon rolled. Pretty soon he started
trotting. It was all too much for Ebenezer, who could hardly believe
his nearsighted eyes. He liked being a passenger and was thinking they
ought to take turns in the future.

The wagon was heavy with Ebenezer in it, and before long the pig
had to slow down. There began a creaky, squeaky, whinny-whining of
the wheels as the wagon wheedled along.

They reached Hawthorn Hill about six o'clock, and Farmer Palmer tugged and struggled and jerked and lugged and grunted and wheezed, and his chubby legs grew weaker as he wrestled the wagon up the difficult slope. The reclining Ebenezer watched with pity. "Attapig, Palmer," he said, "you're not doing badly." These words of encouragement helped. They maddened Farmer Palmer just enough to give him strength to reach the top.

There he rested a moment and looked with relief at the downgrade. He would just coast along as the wagon descended of its own weight.

He started off with a leap and suddenly it was all happening too
rapidly. The wagon was hustling him along and his legs were going crazy.
Then he was lifted into the air by the shafts, with his feet churning round
like a whirligig. He was sure he was seeing his last of the world as it
flashed past. Ebenezer brayed his dismay to the encircling heavens and
tried too late to yank on the brake.

There was a bib-bibbidy-rib-ribbidy-*rip* as the wheels ricketed over rocks and ruts and tore loose from the wagon, flying their separate ways. Ebenezer somersaulted backward over the backboard, and Farmer Palmer kissed the ground as the wagon shot over him.

The ass, the pig, and what had once been a wagon were distributed over the hillside.

"Are you all right?" Farmer Palmer inquired.

"It'll take a long time to find out how all right I am," Ebenezer said. "How are you?"

"Everything hurts," said Farmer Palmer, "but nothing seems broken. Except the wagon." They looked at each other and shook their heads. "The wagon can't be fixed," said the pig.

"Not by the world's best wainwrights," said Ebenezer.

"What do we do now?" Farmer Palmer moaned.

"I guess you'll have to carry me," said Ebenezer. "Wait a minute! The bike!" It was lying in a bed of daisies.

"Holy hog!" said Farmer Palmer. "That's it!" He mounted the
bicycle and propelled himself a few yards. "This will do it!" he cried.
"Let's get going!"

Using bits of harness, he fastened the tool chest to the carrier behind
the seat and strapped the camera with its tripod to Ebenezer's back.
Then he straddled the bicycle and waited, hoofs on handlebars, while
Ebenezer climbed aboard and locked him in a safe embrace.

They were both exhausted. Farmer Palmer pedaled with trembly legs and they wibble-wobbled along the road. Ebenezer soon fell asleep on the pig's shoulder, snoring with oaten breath.

"If I could only lay my own weary form on the dear, green ground and sleep like my friend Ebenezer," thought Farmer Palmer. But a vision of the beloved round faces and small sweet eyes of his wife and